On a grim pea-souper of a night, Sherlock Holmes and Dr Watson go missing. Little Ned thinks they've become headless corpses in the river, but Arthur is not convinced. He determines to find them and help solve the baffling investigation they've been conducting.

Where is the belly-button of the great god Dennis? Who is the Burglar with No Feet? Why is the Earl of Stepney's nut-dish empty? What has happened to Dr Watson's kidneys?

These and many more peculiar questions are posed in a mystery that threatens to defeat even the great Sherlock Holmes. Luckily, Arthur helps him out . . .

Alan Coren went to university at Oxford, Yale and Berkeley, California. He was editor of *Punch* for ten years until 1987. He writes for adults and children, and appears regularly on radio and television. He is generally regarded as the funniest man writing in English.

ALAN COREN

ARTHUR
AND THE BELLYBUTTON
DIAMOND

Illustrated by John Astrop

PUFFIN BOOKS

PUFFIN BOOKS

Penguin Books Ltd, 27 Wrights Lane, London W8 5TZ (Publishing and Editorial)
and Harmondsworth, Middlesex, England (Distribution and Warehouse)
Viking Penguin Inc., 40 West 23rd Street, New York, New York 10010, USA
Penguin Books Australia Ltd, Ringwood, Victoria, Australia
Penguin Books Canada Ltd, 2801 John Street, Markham, Ontario, Canada L3R 1B4
Penguin Books (NZ) Ltd, 182–190 Wairau Road, Auckland 10, New Zealand

First published by Robson Books 1979
Published in Puffin Books 1981
Reprinted 1984, 1986, 1988

Copyright © Alan Coren, 1979
All rights reserved

Made and printed in Great Britain by
Richard Clay Ltd, Bungay, Suffolk
Filmset in Monophoto Times

For Nicky

Thick, grey-green, oily-damp, the chill November fog hung heavy over Baker Street. Through it, though it was late morning, few sounds came: the oddly muffled hoof of a cab-horse whose driver was brave or foolish enough to be plying for hire; the occasional tap-tap of a walking stick; far off, the tinny squeak of a beggar's penny whistle; the barking, here and there, of invisible London dogs; and, from time to time, the yell of someone who had walked into a lamp-post.

From his broad bay window upstairs at Number 221B, Sherlock Holmes stared out into the clammy greyness, moodily; his unlit pipe hung from his cheerless mouth, and the brightness in his keen blue eyes was curiously bitter.

'A fine day for villains, Watson!' he burst out

suddenly. 'There is much dirty work being done out there today, invisible to the law!'

Doctor Watson, at the round table beside the crackling fire, merely dug a fork into his sixth kipper.

'The perfect day,' he replied, 'to stay in and eat, Holmes! I say, I've just realized I've polished off your breakfast, too, I really am most awfully –'

Holmes waved a bony hand impatiently.

'I have no appetite,' he snapped. 'There is only one thing I wish to get *my* teeth into, Watson, and that is a nice juicy case. Something with dreadful Oriental villains, perhaps; something with baffling codes to unravel; or a shocking international scandal, Watson, involving grisly headless corpses and –'

'I say, Holmes!' cried Watson. 'Not when a chap's eating!'

Holmes glared at him.

'In that case,' he muttered, 'it is most unlikely that we shall ever be able to hold a serious conversation since there is no time when you are *not* eating!'

'That's most unfair, Holmes,' replied Doctor Watson, slicing the top from his boiled egg, 'I've got to get this breakfast eaten up, it'll be lunchtime before we know it; if I sit around chatting all the time what's going to happen to all these boiled eggs, never mind the toast and marmalade?'

Whether Sherlock Holmes intended to ignore

this, or whether he would have preferred to throw his pipe at Doctor Watson, we shall never know. For at that very moment, there was a thunderous

noise of hurrying boots upon the staircase outside, followed by an even more thunderous knocking at the door.

'Aha!' cried Sherlock Holmes, his face suddenly brightening. 'Something would appear to be up! Come in, Inspector.'

The door opened, and Inspector Lestrade of Scotland Yard burst breathlessly into the room. As always, his dark face bristled with suspicion.

'How,' he bellowed, 'did you know it was me?'

Sherlock Holmes smiled.

'Once I have heard a boot,' he murmured, 'I never forget it. A footstep, my dear Lestrade, is as individual as a finger-print. I have written three short books upon the subject, and I keep in my head the clear memory of some sixteen hundred and thirty-two feet.'

'Amazing,' mumbled Watson, through a large piece of smoked ham.

'Elementary,' said Holmes. 'If you remember, Watson, the case of the Giant Ferret of White-chapel, you may recall that I identified the murderer from the noise of his left sock.'

Watson burped, but in a very gentlemanly manner.

'I wonder,' he murmured, delicately picking a toast crumb from his moustache, 'whether Mrs Hudson has any kidneys up her sleeve?'

'Kidneys!' cried Inspector Lestrade, with such force that the plates piled around Doctor Watson jumped and rattled. 'The Earl of Stepney's diamond tiepin 'as been stolen, nicked, knocked off, and generally, not to put too fine a point on it, pinched, and all you can talk about is bloomin' kidneys?'

The eagerness which had recently flushed Sherlock Holmes's thin cheeks suddenly paled.

'A tiepin?' he muttered. He walked stiffly to the window, hands clasped behind his back, and said, without turning his head, 'I do not do tiepins. Nor, Inspector,' and his voice was strangely tight, 'do I do lost umbrellas, criminals suspected of travelling without a bus-ticket, or, for that matter, cats stuck up trees.'

Doctor Watson waved a forkful of smoked haddock at Lestrade.

'You've upset him now, Inspector,' he said. 'You seem to forget that Mr Holmes is the greatest detective in the world.'

'That's as maybe,' snapped Lestrade, who preferred to think of Sherlock Holmes as the *second* greatest detective in the world, 'but this is no ordinary tiepin, neither.'

'*Either*,' Holmes corrected, though in a polite murmur. He turned around. 'And what, Inspector, makes this tiepin so extraordinary?'

'It 'appens to contain,' replied Lestrade, 'the Bellybutton Diamond!'

The effect of this upon Sherlock Holmes was remarkable!

'What!' he exclaimed, 'But that is the largest diamond in the world! And surely it belongs to the Akond of Swat?'

'Who, or why, or which, or what,' inquired Doctor Watson, 'is the Akond of Swat?'

'He is a great South American ruler beloved of his people,' answered Inspector Lestrade. 'Or was.'

'You mean he's dead?' asked Watson.

'No, I mean he's not beloved any more. They did not like 'im unscrewing the belly-button of their god, Dennis, and selling it to the Earl of Stepney. See, the Akond of Swat is barmy about clockwork trains. Can't get enough of 'em. I

11

understand 'e has converted the top floor of his palace into a replica of Dalston Junction – eighty-eight miles of track, sixty-one engines, four hundred and twenty-two ...'

'Oh, get on with it!' shouted Holmes, who, sensing the case was somewhat more curious than he had at first imagined, had grown very impatient. 'Everyone knows what Dalston Junction looks like.'

'Speak for yourself, Holmes,' protested Watson. 'Personally, I've never got further than its dining-room. Go on, Inspector.'

'Well, clockwork trains cost money, I don't have to tell you that, and the Akond was running a bit short last year. So he looked around for something to sell, and he reckoned this big marble statue of Dennis outside Swat town hall didn't need a diamond belly-button, so 'e unscrewed it and flogged it to the Earl of Stepney. Who 'ad it made into a tiepin.'

'Curiouser and curiouser!' muttered Sherlock Holmes (whose favourite book was *Alice in Wonderland*). He began to pace up and down. 'It is my understanding that the Bellybutton Diamond is the size of a man's fist. How on earth can the Earl of Stepney wear it on his tie?'

'With great difficulty,' replied Lestrade. ''E is only a little bloke, and 'is head keeps getting dragged forward with the weight. But 'e's got his reasons for wearing it, Mr Holmes, and very

12

peculiar reasons they are, too, I don't mind saying.'

'You will have to explain them in the cab,' cried Holmes, snatching his cape and deerstalker hat from their pegs. 'There is no time to be lost, Inspector! We must hurry to the scene of what I fear may turn out to be a very terrible crime indeed!'

But as he and Lestrade waited somewhat irritably while Doctor Watson eased his podgy bulk away from the breakfast table and struggled into his enormous coat and wrapped some cold sausages in his napkin for the journey, more foot-steps sounded outside, followed by a polite knock.

'Who's this, Holmes?' said Watson.

Holmes frowned.

'I've no idea,' he replied. 'The shoes are entirely unfamiliar.'

He pulled the door open.

A small boy stood there. He raised his hat politely.

'Good morning, Mr Holmes,' said Arthur.

'Good morning, Arthur,' said the great detective. 'You have new shoes, I hear.'

Arthur nodded.

'And you, Mr Holmes,' he said, 'are about to call on the Earl of Stepney.'

'Good heavens!' cried Watson. 'However did you know that?'

''E prob'ly listens at key 'oles,' muttered Lestrade, who did not like small boys.

'Come, come, my dear Inspector,' said Sherlock Holmes sternly, 'you know Arthur better than that.'

'Humph!' humphed the policeman. For he *did* know Arthur better than that; which was half the trouble, because he had met Arthur, as those of you who have read *Arthur and the Great Detective*

may remember, on board the S.S. *Murgatroyd*, when Arthur had managed to solve a remarkably tricky crime that had baffled not only Inspector Lestrade, which was to be expected, but also Sherlock Holmes, which was not. And while Holmes was a generous person who was delighted that a small boy had succeeded where he had failed, Inspector Lestrade was a rather small-minded person, who hated being outdone, particularly by children.

So he said to Arthur now:

'Well then, clever dick, if you *wasn't* listening at key 'oles, 'ow, may I ask, did you know about the Earl of Stepney?'

'Because,' said Arthur, 'at nine o'clock this morning, I learned that the Bellybutton Diamond had been stolen, so I –'

'But,' cried the agitated Lestrade, 'the police themselves didn't find out till nine-fifteen! A small boy run all the way with the message!'

'*Ran* all the way,' corrected Arthur, even more quietly and politely than Sherlock Holmes had done. 'Yes, he did. He was one of my Baker Street Irregulars.'

'And what,' snorted Lestrade scornfully, 'might *they* be when they're at home?'

'When they're at home,' replied Arthur, 'they're just small boys. But when they're out and about the streets of London for me and Mr Holmes, they're detectives and spies and messengers and almost anything you care to think of. We're a network, aren't we, Mr Holmes?'

'That you are, Arthur,' nodded the great detective, 'and a most valuable one. There is much that an unobtrusive small boy may see and hear, Lestrade, that a large and, er, noisy policeman may not. Such as the first news of the Bellybutton Diamond affair, eh, Arthur? But come, we are wasting valuable time! Arthur, since you were in at the start of things you had better accompany us to Stepney Castle.'

15

'Right!' said Arthur. 'I'll just fetch my magnifying glass.'

Inspector Lestrade rolled his eyes.

'And how long will *that* take?' he groaned.

'Only a moment,' replied Arthur. 'I live upstairs.'

'Upstairs?' echoed Lestrade. 'You mean at –'

'221A,' said Arthur.

Outside, the dank fog folded them in. Even to one another, standing close, they became little

more than silhouettes, four oddly assorted shapes in the silent swirling gloom. It must be like this under the sea, thought Arthur. Above them, a gaslight hung, strangely disembodied from its post by the fog and still glowing yellow, the lamplighter having not yet come by, because of the weather, to turn it out. Its light was worse than none at all; it shed an eeriness, distorting shadows, conjuring odd visions in the shifting veils of fog.

'There will be murders today,' murmured Sherlock Holmes.

'Blow murders!' cried Doctor Watson, stout and cheery as ever. 'Will there be cabs, is what *I* want to know?'

As if in answer, an unseen hoof crunched on a cobble, an invisible wheel-rim rasped, iron against stone: a second later, a horse's head appeared, like an apparition, floating above them, nostril-steam pluming into the fog. Sherlock Holmes took a quick step forward and banged his cane against the cab's flank. The cabbie stopped, leaned down, not much more than a smile and a bit of top hat. Just like the Cheshire cat, thought Arthur (his favourite book was *Alice in Wonderland*, too).

'Stepney Castle,' called Holmes, 'quick as you can!'

He opened the hansom's door.

'We'll never all get in there,' complained Lestrade. 'It only seats two at the best of times.'

'But these,' muttered Holmes, climbing inside, 'are the worst of times. Still, if you'd prefer to wait for another, Inspector, I dare say – '

'Oh, very well!' snapped the policeman, who had no intention of being left alone in the fog. A hundred years ago, London was a rather more dangerous place than it is today. Policemen went about in pairs, if they were wise. If they were not, they tended to be found next morning, floating face downwards in the icy Thames.

So Arthur squeezed into a corner, and Lestrade sat on Doctor Watson's lap; which, if it did little for his dignity, at least did more for it than if the enormous Watson had been sitting on *his* lap. Thus packed together, bouncing gently as the poorly sprung wheels clacked over the cobbles, they were borne up Baker Street, along Marylebone Road, and away from fashionable London towards the older, darker, grimmer East End.

Not that they saw much of it. The fog showed no signs of thinning; as they passed the great stations of Euston and King's Cross, only the hoot and hiss of engines and the crunch of shunted wagons gave them their bearings, and as they clip-clopped up Pentonville Road, it was the guards calling to one another as they nervously patrolled the huge walls that reminded Holmes of the great

18

prison that lay only a few yards away through the impenetrable gloom.

'There are a few lads over there, Lestrade,' he said nodding, 'who'd like to get their hands around our throats, eh? Let's hope they've remembered to shoot the bolts! It'd be no bad day to escape, and settle a few old scores!'

At which the unhappy Inspector, bouncing on Watson's fat knee like an irritable baby, shuddered from hat to boot.

'Oh, by the way, Lestrade,' Holmes continued, 'I believe you were going to explain what you were pleased to call the peculiar reasons why the Earl of Stepney struggled around in this enormous diamond tiepin of his?'

19

'Correct,' replied the policeman, though the word actually came out as a hiccup, since they had just jolted over a particularly nasty pot-hole. 'The Earl of Stepney is what might be termed dead common. 'E is not a gent. 'E was formerly Wilfred Nutt of Tooting, until 'e inherited the title by accident last year.'

'By accident?' inquired Doctor Watson's puffed voice from under the Inspector.

'Right. Last Christmas, the previous Earl of Stepney, who was as posh a nob as you could shake a stick at and was widely known as someone who never ate peas off his knife, invited 'is entire family down to 'is place in the country. Entire, that is, except for Wilfred Nutt of Tooting, 'is nineteenth cousin twice removed, and the reason *he* wasn't invited was on account of 'is appalling manners, no doubt picked up at the London Zoo.'

'Zoo?' inquired Holmes.

'I'm coming to that,' said Lestrade. 'So there they all were, two 'undred and fourteen relatives of the Earl of Stepney, about to sit down to a full turkey dinner, when it snowed.'

Here, the Inspector paused dramatically. He was enjoying himself, as he always did on those very few occasions when he happened to know something which Sherlock Holmes did not. He waited a few seconds, then went on:

'So the Earl of Stepney suddenly suggested they

all go outside for a bit of a skate on the ornamental lake until dinner was ready.'

'I see,' murmured Sherlock Holmes. 'How dreadful!'

'Quite,' nodded Lestrade. 'Odd thing is, the ice would've held two hundred and thirteen relatives: it was only when the two hundred and fourteenth stepped on to it that it finally cracked. One minute they was all whizzing around on it, the next there was just this big black 'ole with a lot of smart hats bobbing about.'

'Tragic,' muttered Sherlock Holmes.

'Shocking,' agreed the Inspector. 'They 'ad to throw away eighteen roast turkeys, not to mention six 'undred mince pies. And as for all them brussels sprouts, well –'

'So that left Wilfred Nutt of Tooting as the only surviving relative,' exclaimed Doctor Watson, 'and thus the new Earl!'

'And 'im nothing more nor less,' said Lestrade, 'than the man what cleaned the elephants' toenails up the London Zoo! Imagine that – one day you're earning ten bob a week picking yesterday's breakfast out of an elephant's big toe, the next you're a bloomin' earl. Well, it went to 'is head, didn't it?'

'How, exactly?' asked Sherlock Holmes, keenly.

'Soon as 'e heard,' answered Lestrade, 'he threw his broom and toenail clippers at the Head Elephant Keeper, and walked out. A week later, he was back, new yellow suit, new blue shirt, new green tie and matching bowler 'at – and in the middle of that tie ...'

'The biggest diamond in the world,' finished Sherlock Holmes, nodding and narrowing his eyes.

'Right! 'E just sat there all morning, watching 'em clean the elephants out, and laughing all over his bloomin' face! And of course,' Lestrade went on, 'they couldn't say nothing, could they, not with 'im being an earl. They just 'ad to grit their teeth and bear it. Even when he threw 'em buns.'

'The elephants?' inquired Watson.

'The keepers!' cried the Inspector. 'Just to rub their faces in it. I told you 'e was dead common, didn't I?'

The cab stopped.

Holmes peered into the fog, which was thinning slightly, now, and exclaimed:

'Good heavens! They appear to be knocking Stepney Castle down!'

It was true. As the four descended from the cab, they could hardly hear themselves think for the noise of sledge-hammers and falling brickwork. Even as they stared, one huge turreted tower of Stepney Castle shuddered, split, and came crashing down almost at their feet, the choking brick dust swirling up around them.

'The clues!' shouted Holmes, when he had finished coughing. 'All the clues will be utterly destroyed!'

'Wrong!' cried Inspector Lestrade, delighted, of course, to know something which the great detective didn't.

'I beg your pardon?' said Holmes.

'The Earl doesn't live in Stepney Castle any more,' said Arthur. 'He sold it to pay for the Bellybutton Diamond. They're knocking it down and building a tram station.'

Lestrade glared at him.

'I was just going to say that,' he muttered angrily.

'The Bellybutton Diamond,' continued Arthur, 'was stolen from 14, Pondicherry Villas. That's where the Earl lives now; it's just around the corner, if you'd like to follow me, Mr Holmes.'

Whereupon Arthur set off smartly into the lightening fog, with Sherlock Holmes at his heels and Doctor Watson and Lestrade bringing up the rear.

'I shall 'ave to do something about that boy,' said the Inspector grimly.

'Yes,' said Doctor Watson, nodding, 'he's being jolly helpful, isn't he? I say, why not buy him a Dundee Cake? He'd never be able to finish it all himself, of course, but I should be more than happy to help out with a slice or . . .'

'Oh, shut up!' muttered Lestrade, who had grown so irritable that he forgot to salute the constable on the gate as they turned in at 14, Pondicherry Villas. With the rather interesting result that the constable, PC Filge, became so depressed at being ignored that he resigned from the Force at the end of that week, invented the Filge

Portable Bath, and subsequently became the second richest man in Bermondsey.

Victorian England was a land of great opportunity for people prepared to roll their sleeves up and work hard.

Not that the new Earl of Stepney could be described as one of them. When the keen quartet knocked on his modest front door, a very old butler showed them in and took them straight up the cabbage-smelly stairs to the front bedroom. The Earl was in bed, with a tin basin of soapy water beside him, blowing bubbles.

'I never 'ad much time for soap,' was the first thing he said, 'but you 'ave to admit that when it comes to blowing bubbles, it don't half come in 'andy. 'Ave you found my diamond?'

'I'm afraid not, your Grace,' replied Lestrade, bowing low, as he always did when sucking up to important people. 'But this is the famous detective

Mr Sherlock Holmes and his, er, distinguished colleague, Doctor Watson, and I 'ave no doubt that with a little help from them, I shall be able to recover your diamond in double-quick ...'

'What's that other thing?' cried the Earl of Stepney shrilly, pointing a bony hand very rudely indeed.

Lestrade coughed.

'That is a boy, your Grace,' he replied, 'in a manner of speaking.'

'I thought it was!' shrieked the Earl, the red bobble on his grubby night-cap bouncing furiously. 'I can tell boy a mile off! They used to be all over my Zoo, boys. I'd have fed 'em all to the lions, if I'd 'ad my way. Go down a treat, minced boy. Lot better off inside a lion than running about the Zoo with their great muddy boots, pulling faces at the bears, leaving toffee papers everywhere. Never could stand boy! What's he doing on my premises?'

'He is with me,' snapped Sherlock Holmes, very sternly. 'He is Arthur, my personal assistant.'

'Well, don't let 'im touch nothing,' barked the Earl. 'It's bad enough moving into this poky blooming house without having a lot of boys putting their sticky fingers on the wallpaper.'

'Since you mention it,' Holmes remarked, 'might I ask why you sold a perfectly respectable castle just in order to buy a somewhat ostentatious, not to say extremely uncomfortable, tiepin?'

The awful little Earl rolled his eyes.

'Calls himself a detective!' he snorted. 'Did it ever occur to you that you can't go out wearing a castle?'

'I see,' murmured Holmes. 'You wished people to know at once that you were a very rich man. Rather unwise, was it not?'

'None of your business!' snapped the Earl. 'You just get on with finding it. I am not moving out of this bed till I get my diamond back.'

The Earl appeared to think that was some kind of threat; but, thought Arthur privately, it would probably be no great loss to the world if the Earl of Stepney were to stay in bed blowing bubbles for the rest of his life.

'Well, then,' said Sherlock Holmes, 'since you, sir, have chosen to inform the whole of London that the world's most valuable diamond is readily available to anyone who cares to break into your premises, I must lose no further time in examining the scene of the crime. Come, gentlemen!'

And Holmes, Watson, and Arthur hurried out, leaving Inspector Lestrade to tell the Earl of Stepney what an extraordinarily attractive night-cap he was wearing, what magnificent bubbles he was blowing, and so on. Keep on the right side of earls, said Inspector Lestrade to himself, you could wake up one morning and find yourself *Chief* Inspector.

Downstairs, Holmes closed one eye and let the

other sweep slowly around the little sitting-room.

'It was here, I understand, that the robbery took place,' he said to the butler.

'Right, sir,' said the butler, who was about a hundred years old, and wore a mildewed tail-coat.

His name was Squeebs, and it was so long since anyone had called him by his Christian name that he had now forgotten it completely. He had been a butler since 1805, when his first job had been to go upstairs and tell the Duchess of Clacton that Lord Nelson had been killed at the Battle of Trafalgar and would not now be coming down for the weekend, and could he therefore have Saturday off to go and see his Auntie Maureen in Camberwell?

'Where were you at the time?' inquired Holmes.

'I was sleeping in the room next door,' replied Squeebs. 'His Lordship always liked to leave his

tiepin on the mantelpiece in here, just in case anyone dropped in and he needed to point it out to
them, so I had to sleep downstairs, next door to it,
to prevent it from being,' and here the poor old
butler dropped his already quiet voice, 'stolen.'

'Pretty rotten plan, as it turned out!' exclaimed
Doctor Watson.

Squeebs looked at him wretchedly.

'It's the legs, sir,' he said. 'I mean, I woke up all
right when I heard the burglar, but by the time
I'd got these old legs of mine working, and the
door unlocked, he'd gone.'

Sherlock Holmes, who had been peering at the
mantelpiece through his magnifying glass, spun
round.

'You *heard* the burglar?' he cried.

Squeebs nodded.

'As a matter of fact,' he said, 'he was shouting
for cheese.'

This time it was Arthur's turn to put down his
magnifying glass and gasp.

'Why on earth should a burglar shout for cheese,
Mr Squeebs?' he said.

'I'm sure I couldn't say,' replied Squeebs, looking sadder than ever.

'Well, *I* could!' said Doctor Watson firmly.
'Most natural thing in the world to fancy a nice
piece of cheese in the middle of the night. Fre-
quently do it myself. Nice firm yellow slab of cheddar, or a lovely smelly chunk of gorgonzola, or a –'

29

'Oh, for heaven's sake, Watson!' interrupted Holmes. 'We must assume that there were two of them, and they said something to one another which Mr Squeebs mistakenly overheard as cheese. You have not touched anything here, I take it? Good. In that case, is there anything we should take particular notice of, Arthur?'

'Are you referring to the Brazil nuts, Mr Holmes?'

The great detective smiled warmly.

'Precisely, my dear fellow! Perhaps Mr Squeebs can tell us why the grate should be full of Brazil nutshells?'

The old butler shook his bald and wrinkled head. Looks not unlike a Brazil nut himself, thought Arthur, though of course he said nothing.

'I've no idea, sir. They weren't there when I went to bed. I'd just cleaned the room. But the nut-dish on the sideboard's empty.'

'I should think that about wraps it up, then,' announced Watson. 'We are clearly dealing with a burglar who likes eating nuts and cheese. Narrows the field down a lot, doesn't it, Holmes? Burglar with jolly peculiar eating habits, if you ask me. Won't be hard to find.'

Sherlock Holmes quite properly ignored this. There were rather more important facts to be established. He pointed his walking stick at the windows.

'Bars,' muttered Holmes.

'And Mr Squeebs said the door was locked on the outside,' said Arthur.

'Quite,' said Holmes. He smiled a quizzical little smile, which he always did when things became interesting. 'We would appear to have found ourselves an intriguing little problem, Arthur. We have barred windows, the bars screwed firmly in and not apparently disturbed, and we have a door locked from the outside. And yet we also have two vanished criminals. The windows themselves were open, I take it, Mr Squeebs?'

The butler nodded.

'Then, Arthur,' said Sherlock Holmes, 'I believe I have no need to tell you our next move. Come, Watson, let us go outside. Mr Squeebs, would you be so good as to accompany us?'

By the time the three men had reached the little front garden, Arthur was sitting outside on the window-sill.

'Good Lord!' exclaimed Doctor Watson. 'How did you manage that?'

'With some difficulty, I should imagine,' said Sherlock Holmes. 'Am I correct, Arthur?'

Arthur nodded. His shirt was torn, and he was panting heavily.

'I almost didn't manage it,' he said. 'If I'd been half an inch broader, I'd have got stuck in the bars.'

'So boys did it!' breathed Squeebs. '*Boys!* His Lordship will go barmy when he hears.'

31

'Let us not jump to conclusions,' said Sherlock
Holmes. 'It is not my experience that small boys
go around stealing diamonds.'

'There's something else,' said Arthur. 'May I
draw your attention to the curious matter of the
footprints?'

Doctor Watson peered through the misty air at
the khaki patch of garden.

'But there *are* no footprints!' he exclaimed.

'That,' replied Arthur, 'is the curious matter. I
was jolly careful not to jump down from this
window-sill. But if I'd wanted to, there's no way
I could have done it without leaving my footprints

in all this wet mud. Now, how do you suppose the burglars managed to get away without getting down, Mr Holmes?'

Holmes did not answer. He took out his pipe, and filled it from his leather pouch, and lit it slowly. At last he said:

'These are deep waters, Arthur. Burglars who call for cheese while pursuing their crime, burglars who leave nothing behind them but nutshells, burglars who are small enough to squeeze between iron bars – but above all, gentlemen, burglars who would appear to have no feet!'

'HA!' thundered a voice. 'If that's the conclusion you've got to, Mr 'Olmes, we might 'ave saved ourselves the cab-fare!'

Inspector Lestrade stood on the path behind them, stocky legs astride, a typical cocky sneer upon his face. Sherlock Holmes sighed heavily.

'Our investigations, my dear Lestrade,' he said, 'have hardly begun. Though, of course, I take it that you yourself have not been idle? From the soapy water on your sleeves, down your waistcoat, and even now dripping from your moustache, would I be correct in assuming that you have been blowing bubbles?'

The Inspector's black bushy eyebrows shook, but he said nothing.

'Sometimes,' murmured Sherlock Holmes, 'I have grave doubts about the future of the Metropolitan Police Force.' He buttoned his Inverness cape against the bitter day. 'But come along, Arthur, you may get down from the window-sill now, we have other fish to fry!'

'Hurrah!' cried Doctor Watson. 'I wondered whether you'd all forgotten about lunch!'

'It's merely an expression, Watson!' snapped Holmes irritably. 'We have things to do before lunch, if we are to earn our food.'

Arthur jumped down into the garden; but he did not join his friends.

'If it's all right with you, Mr Holmes,' he said, 'I'd like to take another look at the room. You go on without me.'

'As you wish, Arthur, but' – and here the great detective smiled one of those smiles that even the kindliest adults sometimes use on small boys – 'I think you're probably wasting your time. I myself have examined the scene of the crime very thoroughly indeed.'

Whereupon he and Watson and Lestrade melted together into the greyness. Only Squeebs remained, shuffling back up the garden path.

'Just a very quick look, please, Mr Squeebs,' said Arthur.

The ancient butler sighed.

'All right, but don't make a *sound*. If his Lordship thought there was a boy running around the house alone, I really don't know what would become of us both. Bury us under the rockery, I shouldn't wonder.'

He mumbled away, shaking his head. Arthur stepped quickly into the sitting-room. Where, very quickly and very tidily, he opened every drawer and cupboard, searched every surface, looked under every chair and even behind every ornament and picture.

'I thought so,' he murmured quietly as he closed the door again. 'There are no nutcrackers.'

As Arthur turned into Regent's Park, the winter evening was already beginning to fall. The fog had thickened again, as fogs will, and it crossed his mind that this might not perhaps be the best of evenings to take his usual short cut across the park to Baker Street.

It was peculiar, walking through the dropping darkness with all around him the echoing noises of the wild animals from the Zoo which stood at the park's heart: here, on a cold English evening, he could hear the roaring bellow of the lions, the high chatter of the apes, the shriek and gibber of a thousand different voices which had been transported here from half a world away.

Arthur, though he was very brave, shuddered. Just as his great friend Sherlock Holmes had that morning wondered what might happen to him if the dangerous criminals escaped from Pentonville Prison, so Arthur in his turn was forced to think about the possible consequences if the animals burst out of the Zoo, vanished into the fog unnoticed by the keepers, and, padding on silent feet, licking invisible lips, suddenly ...

You could get eaten here, in the middle of London, thought Arthur, and no one would ever know. He quickened his steps.

It was as he was crossing the little ironwork bridge that straddled the Regent's Canal that Arthur suddenly felt – he did not quite know how – that he was not alone. There was no street-light on the bridge, no friendly glow of gas; he stopped, in what was by now the pitch blackness. There was no sound; the fog muffled the distant traffic, and suddenly, queerly, the animals had fallen utterly silent.

He could see absolutely nothing. He could hear absolutely nothing. But he knew, with an awful prickling of the skin, that there was something more than absolutely nothing very, very close to him.

And then:

Arthur was running for his life even before the echoes of the terrible shout had died! He ran with his lungs bursting and his heart hammering, headlong through the terrible blackness. For that voice was no ordinary voice, and that cry was no ordinary cry – it was the exact same cry that Squeebs the butler had heard burst from the throat of the villains who had made away with the Earl of Stepney's diamond!

Had they seen him at the house? Hidden invisible in the fog, and followed him, to kill him in the blackness of the park? Had they – and here, suddenly, an idea began to form in Arthur's mind, an idea that seemed to pump new energy into his pounding, tired feet, an idea that hurled him on towards Baker Street, an idea that he had to give to Sherlock Holmes before it was too –

37

There was a light!

Glowing in the fog, the first lamp-light of Baker Street; and Arthur threw himself, gasping, out of the park at last, daring for the first time to glance behind him.

There was nobody there.

He ran on, but more slowly now, for there were people in the streets, and lit windows, and strolling policemen, and shouting newsboys, and clattering cabs, and the general hum and hubbub of London.

In short, there was safety. Above all, there was 221B.

But when he arrived, he was surprised to see no warm light from Sherlock Holmes's bay window softening the fog. It was, after all, well past Doctor Watson's tea-time; and Arthur knew that their housekeeper, Mrs Hudson, was preparing kidneys, a dish for which Doctor Watson would, in normal circumstances, have swum the Channel in his boots and overcoat or run across the boiling Sahara with a sack of bricks under each arm.

Arthur rang the doorbell (he was allowed a key; but, like all the best detectives, never carried it in case he should be captured by villains and the key fall into the wrong hands), and hardly had the chime died before the door was pulled open by a very distressed Mrs Hudson.

'Oh, Master Arthur!' she cried. 'Whatever can have happened to Mr Holmes and Doctor Watson? I mean, Mr Holmes often stays out on account of being on detective work and similar, but Dr Watson never, *never* misses grilled kidneys!'

Arthur closed the door, took Mrs Hudson's arm firmly, and led her to a green velvet chair beside the hallstand, smiling comfortingly: he, of course, was extremely worried, too, but was far too sensible to show it.

'There is absolutely nothing to concern yourself about, Mrs Hudson,' he said. 'There are no two people in this world more capable of looking after themselves than Sherlock Holmes and Doctor Watson.'

But what he thought was: I just hope they're capable *enough*, this time. And, having thought that, Arthur knew exactly what he had to do; so before Mrs Hudson had the chance to try to persuade him against it, Arthur had turned, and was out through the door again and into Baker Street.

Where he walked a few yards to the first corner, cupped his hands around his mouth, and whistled a strange whistle, clear and high, hoping that it was not so late that no one would hear.

He did not need to whistle a second time; a half-minute later, a hand touched his arm. He could just make out the face, as he turned, of Little Ned, tiniest (yet probably toughest, too) of the Baker Street Irregulars. Arthur had guessed that it would be Little Ned who answered the special whistle; for Little Ned never went home when he should have done for the simple reason that his parents never noticed whether he was there or not. This was mainly because Little Ned had sixteen brothers and sisters; and his father and mother, since these were hard times for working-men and education was not what it is today, had never learned to count further than twelve; with the result that they were never quite sure whether all their children were in or not, especially as they were very poor, and could afford only one candle per night.

So Little Ned was almost always about when Arthur needed him.

'Wot's up, Arfur?' asked Little Ned.

'Holmes and Watson,' replied Arthur grimly. 'They're missing.'

'Been done in,' said Little Ned, even more grimly. 'It's been one of them days, Arfur. Bet the river's full of stiffs tonight. Bet there's corpses all over. 'Eadless, too, I shouldn't wonder. Bet there's bodies all over Hyde Park with Chinese knives sticking out of their backs. Bet the trees

down 'Ackney Marshes 'as got a thousand dead
'uns hanging off 'em. Yes, no doubt about it,
mate, they've been done in.'

'It's possible,' said Arthur; because it was, even
though Little Ned had always had a somewhat
gory imagination. 'But in case they haven't, it's
our job to find them. And you're just the one to
put us on the right track!'

'Cab shelter?' inquired Little Ned.

'Right first time!' cried Arthur.

Because Little Ned's father was a cabman;
which meant that Little Ned knew all the cab-
drivers, who would tell Little Ned things they
would not tell any ordinary small boy. So together
Little Ned and Arthur hurried through the damp
darkness to the big green hut at the corner of
Marylebone Lane where the cabbies came on
winter nights to unfreeze their bones around the

roaring fire, and unchill their blood with hot tea and rum.

'Best go in alone,' said Little Ned, when they arrived, and he slipped quickly inside, while Arthur sat on the cold step and stamped his feet against the icy night.

In five minutes, Little Ned reappeared, framed briefly in the oblong of golden light, before the shelter-door slammed shut again.

'Got it!' he cried. 'Bert 'Ancock picked 'em up from Pondicherry Villas about one o'clock. Took 'em to ... Know where 'e took 'em?'

Arthur could feel that, in the darkness, Little Ned was grinning.

'Of course not,' he replied.

'To the circus!' shouted Little Ned. 'What do you think of *that*?'

Arthur gasped.

'I think,' he replied, 'that Mr Holmes and Doctor Watson are in very great danger indeed! There's only one circus in town, Little Ned, and Mr Holmes took me to see it last Saturday, and there was an amazing troupe of South American acrobats called The Astounding Swatties, and if Sherlock Holmes has been putting two and two together, then ... we must get over to Clapham Common right away!'

'But it's six miles to Clapham,' protested Little Ned, 'it'll take all night.'

'Not by cab,' replied Arthur firmly, and pulled

open the door of the cab-shelter again. 'Herbert Hancock!' he shouted. 'Clapham Common, if you please, and drive like the wind!'

Now, Herbert Hancock might have pointed out that he was drinking his cocoa, and he might have pointed out that it was a nasty night, and he might have pointed out that it was long past a small boy's bedtime, and indeed all these replies and more did occur to him, until the golden sovereign in Arthur's fingers caught the light, and Herbert Hancock's eye. So he snatched his whip from the corner, and he jammed his top hat firmly on his huge bald head, and he sprang through the door to his waiting hansom, and five seconds later the cab was hurtling down Wigmore Street at a very illegal gallop, taking the corners on one

clattering wheel, while the two boys inside were thrown about like dice in an egg-cup. Every moment, Arthur and Little Ned expected to find themselves smashed against some sudden obstacle

43

looming out of the black fog, but by a mixture of great good luck and Herbert Hancock's legendary skill, not to mention the extraordinary sixth sense of his horse Tiddles (Mrs Hancock had always wanted a cat), within five short minutes they were thundering over Westminister Bridge, south towards Clapham.

Fairy lights hung winking in the bare trees of the broad common, their colour diffused by the fog so that the air seemed full of coloured powder-puffs. And at the centre of this square of soft colour stood the big top of Chubley's Magic Circus; as Arthur and Little Ned sprinted towards it across the wet grass, they could hear the brassy bellow of steam-organ music and the excited roar of the crowd, and though that might be just the sort of noise most people would *want* to hear coming from a circus tent, the sounds filled Arthur with despair.

'The show's started,' he cried, panting, to Little Ned, 'we may be too late!'

They skidded to a stop at the entrance.

'Two tickets,' said the clown at the ticket table, 'that'll be fourpence, and I'll blow you a free raspberry!'

'We must see The Astounding Swatties,' shouted Arthur, 'before they go on!'

'*Before* they go on?' said the clown, raising his purple eyebrows. His spotted bow-tie revolved in surprise. 'Bit late for that, sonny. They're on now.'

'Oh, no!' cried Arthur. He slapped four pennies down on the wooden table, and raced inside with Little Ned at his heels.

The clown watched them go, gloomily.

'Didn't even wait for my raspberry,' he sniffed. 'Wish I was as popular as them blooming Swatties. Nobody cares about clowns no more.'

He took out a huge red handkerchief, waited for his white rabbit to jump out of it, and blew his nose fiercely.

Inside the enormous tent, Arthur and Little Ned didn't look for seats; they ran straight down to the ringside of the huge sawdust oval, just in time to hear the ringmaster roar:

'AND NOW, THOSE FIVE INCREDIBLE
ARTISTES FROM THE STEAMING JUNGLES OF
SWAT WILL PERFORM THEIR WORLD FAMOUS
FINALE! YES, THAT INCREDIBLE, DEATH-
DEFYING STUNT THAT NO ONTHER ACROBATIC
TEAM HAS DARED EVEN TO *TRY*! LADIES AND
GENTLEMEN. THE ASTOUNDING SWATTIES
WILL SIMULTANEOUSLY FIRE NOT ONE, BUT
TWO MEN FROM THE GIANT CANNONS YOU
SEE BEFORE YOU! LADIES, COVER YOUR
EYES! GENTLEMEN, HOLD YOUR BREATH!
CHUBLEY'S MAGIC CIRCUS IS PROUD AND
PRIVILEGED TO PRESENT – THE DOUBLE
HUMAN CANNONBALL!'

The huge crowd fell suddenly silent.

Except, that is, for Little Ned. Because Little
Ned could count rather better than his parents;

46

which is why he nudged Arthur, and hissed:

''Ere, Arfur, there's not five of 'em. There's seven!'

And Arthur nodded grimly.

For before he could move, or cry out, or do any-thing to stop the dreadful deed that was about to take place, The Astounding Swatties had loaded their cannons with the two extra figures that had been carried on, bound and masked, lit the short fuses, and jumped back.

There was an ear-bursting double explosion, the two cannons leapt on their wheels, *and Sherlock Holmes and Doctor Watson flew up towards the distant roof of the tent!*

As Arthur gazed, horror-stricken, his two friends spun in the arc-lights, going higher, and higher, and higher. And just when he thought they were going to burst through the canvas a hundred feet above and disappear in fragments into the night, they began to fall back towards the ground.

'They'll be smashed to bits!' shouted Little Ned.

But they weren't.

For while the two human cannonballs had been hurtling upwards, with every eye in the audience upon them, The Astounding Swatties had hurriedly and expertly opened out a safety net, running off in five directions, each with a corner, until the net was stretched tight, a few feet above the ground, and it was into this net that Holmes and Watson at last fell, to be lowered gently to the sawdust.

As the cheering thundered out, Arthur and Little Ned jumped the ringside barrier and dashed to the centre of the ring, where their two friends were staggering to their feet, pulling off the masks and ropes, with a little help from the Swatties. They were shaken, but apparently unhurt.

'Mr Holmes!' cried Arthur, 'Doctor Watson! Are you all right?'

''Course them is all right!' grunted a tiny bearded Swattie. Arthur looked at him, and realized for the first time that the Swatties, though fully grown, were little bigger than he was. 'We just teach them big lesson,' he continued. 'We teach them not to go about saying Swatties is criminals.'

Holmes nodded gravely, as the other Swatties – together, it must be said, with Doctor Watson, who had quite recovered – took their bows.

'I'm afraid I made a very big mistake, Arthur,' murmured the great detective, as the mob of Swatties, English gentlemen, and small boys, made for the exit.

'Is true,' said the bearded Swattie. 'Dis man say we pinch diamond belly-button from Dennis de God. Him very lucky we not shooting him at brick wall!'

'I didn't quite say *that*,' protested Sherlock Holmes. 'I said I thought you'd taken it back from the Earl of Stepney because you were angry about the Akond of Swat selling it and wanted to take it home again to Swat. You see, Arthur,' and here he turned to his small friend, 'when I realized that only a very small person could have got through those bars, my first thought – knowing that the people of Swat were no bigger than English boys – was that *they* had repossessed the diamond.

Then, when we noticed no footprints, I eliminated all the other possibilities and deduced that only an acrobat, leaping from the window-sill into the garden's trees, could have escaped leaving no trace. And remembering that we'd seen The Astounding Swatties last week at the circus, I came to the only possible conclusion.'

'Wrong!' cried the bearded acrobat. 'You *jump* to the only *im*possible conclusion!'

And here, as if to make his point, he turned a splendid double somersault.

'Quite,' said Holmes, laughing (which he rarely did). 'So when I accused them, they first proved that they hadn't left their caravan all night, and *then* ...'

'... they tied us up and shoved us in the cannons!' cried Doctor Watson. He smiled broadly. 'Serves us jolly well right!'

'But you ain't hurt?' inquired the bearded Swattie anxiously.

'On the contrary!' cried Doctor Watson. 'The flight has given me an enormous appetite!'

But back at 221B Baker Street, as Doctor Watson tucked belatedly into his grilled kidneys, Sherlock Holmes had become very gloomy again.

For the mystery remained no less mysterious; and the greatest detective in the world had nowhere left to turn for a solution. Which was why, when the polite knock sounded at his door, and the small boy from 221A came into the room in his dressing-gown and slippers, Holmes did not even look up.

'I blame the Brazil nuts,' he muttered, aloud but to himself. 'I asked myself who would have wanted Brazil nuts so much that he stopped during a burglary to eat them, and the inevitable conclusion was: only a South American. It put me on the wrong track, and everything followed from there.'

'I know,' said Arthur. 'Brazil nuts were important; but,' and here he paused, 'so was the cheese.'

Holmes looked up slowly.

'Do you *know* something, Arthur?' he said quietly.

Arthur considered this carefully.

'I *believe* something,' he replied. 'I shan't *know* till tomorrow morning.'

The old light flared up again in Sherlock Holmes's eyes.

'What is it?' he cried.

Arthur grinned. And the grin turned into a yawn.

'It's well past my bedtime, Mr Holmes,' he said. 'And we have to be up early in the morning, if we're to catch these villains of mine!'

Whereupon he said goodnight, went out

smartly, and closed the door behind him. Holmes glared at the door.

'Did you hear what he said, Watson?' he cried. 'Villains of *mine*, indeed! And what, pray, could he possibly know that *I* don't know?'

Doctor Watson wiped a drop of gravy from his moustache.

'He knew enough not to get shot out of a cannon, Holmes,' he said.

'Oh, shut up and finish your kidneys!' snapped Sherlock Holmes.

It was cold in Regent's Park at seven a.m., but the fog had gone. Moisture dripped from the leafless trees. Dawn was just beginning to break, greyly, on the eastern horizon; and as it did so, the outlines of three figures walking quickly through the soaking grass separated themselves from the background of ebbing night.

Sherlock Holmes sneezed, and the echo rattled away across the park. In the distance, a seal, as if in answer, barked.

'I trust,' said Holmes sharply, 'that we are not out in this freezing morning upon some wild goose chase, Arthur.'

'Well,' replied Arthur, 'as a matter of fact, it's a little *like* a wild goose chase.'

Doctor Watson sighed.

'All a bit beyond me, I'm afraid,' he said. He patted his overcoat pocket. 'But I did bring my service revolver, Holmes.'

Arthur, who was leading the little party, turned.

'You won't need it, Doctor,' he said. 'All that's necessary is a nice piece of cheese!'

Whereupon he put his hand in his own coat pocket, and drew out a large slice of yellow cheddar which, as the light grew stronger, he began to wave above his head. And then:

'CHEESE!' shouted Arthur. 'CHEESE!'

The curious echo ran around the park, bouncing off the trees, and wobbling back to them. 'Cheese, cheese, chee . . .'

The next moment, something huge had swooped down out of nowhere and landed on Arthur's shoulder with a piercing cry!

'GIVE US A PIECE OF CHEESE!' shrieked the huge green parrot. 'GIVE US A PIECE OF CHEESE!'

'Good heavens!' exclaimed Doctor Watson.

'The burglar's very words!' cried Sherlock Holmes.

Arthur broke off a piece of cheddar and the parrot dipped neatly and plucked it from his fingers.

'More than that, Mr Holmes,' said Arthur. 'It's the burglar's very voice!'

'You mean – surely not – but how? – but why? – are you telling me that this parrot stole the Bellybutton Diamond?'

'He's telling you himself,' replied Arthur.

'Give us a piece of cheese!' said the parrot again, and Arthur did.

'You see, there were no nutcrackers,' said Arthur, as they watched the big bird gobble happily. 'And I said to myself: no burglar carries his own nutcrackers in the hope of finding Brazil nuts. And no man can crack a Brazil nutshell with his teeth. Some animals could, perhaps, but then what animal would shout for a piece of cheese? There is only one creature on earth,' said Arthur slowly, 'which can both talk *and* crack Brazil nuts!'

'Amazing!' cried Doctor Watson.

'Elementary,' said Arthur modestly. '*And*, of course, it was quite capable of both slipping easily through the bars and getting away without leaving footprints. It simply flew off with the Bellybutton Diamond in its enormous beak. Didn't you?'

'Bellybutton Diamond,' said the parrot. 'Give us a piece of cheese!'

'But why on earth should it suddenly decide to steal a diamond?' asked Sherlock Holmes.

'Oh, it didn't,' replied Arthur. 'Someone else decided. And that someone used what we can all see is a highly trained parrot to do his dirty work for him.'

'How for goodness' sake did you know where to look?' inquired the baffled Doctor Watson.

'Well,' said Arthur, 'it was a matter of deduction. The Earl of Stepney had been showing off his diamond tiepin at the Zoo, hadn't he? And a Zoo is also the sort of place you'd expect to find a parrot, especially a trained one. So I concluded that someone at the Zoo who had a trained parrot had spotted the Bellybutton Diamond and decided to pinch it; and since the parrot is obviously jolly tame and wanders the park, then it's no ordinary caged Zoo parrot, but one that must belong to a Zoo keeper. That's when I decided to take a walk through the park: last evening, I heard the shout in the fog, and I knew for certain what it was all about. All we have to do now is discover the name of his owner; and if the owner *is* a keeper and therefore pretty sensible about animals wandering loose, he'll have put his name on him somewhere.'

And sure enough, as the parrot's claw reached for the last piece of cheddar, Arthur saw the little metal band around its leg. He whipped out his magnifying glass.

*

'Alfred J. Futtergunk,' he read, 'Elephant House, London Zoo.'

They had arrived by now at the Zoo gates. It was quite light,. but the Zoo, said the notice-board, did not open until nine o'clock.

'Nevertheless,' said Sherlock Holmes, producing his visiting-card, 'I rather think we should knock, don't you?'

Alfred J. Futtergunk sat miserably on the stone bench in the Elephant House, and stared at the floor.

'He was always a nasty piece of work, was Wilfred Nutt of Tooting,' he muttered, turning his keeper's hat in his gnarled hands.

'Still is,' declared Doctor Watson. 'Hasn't improved him, becoming an earl.'

'Made him worse,' said Alfred J. Futtergunk.

'Wilfred Nutt of Tooting!' squawked the parrot on his shoulder. 'Nasty!'

'He was bad enough when he worked here,' went on Alfred J. Futtergunk. 'Rude, mean, lazy – used to spend most of his time blowing bubbles, you know. When he wasn't making nasty jokes about people's names. Not that that was important, I'm used to that, but the worst of it was, he was cruel to the elephants.' He turned, and called to the huge quiet animals standing behind him. 'What do you think of Wilfred Nutt of Tooting, then?'

The elephants suddenly opened their eyes, and trumpeted furiously.

'They never forget,' said Alfred J. Futtergunk. He sighed. 'And then after he came into his title and fortune and everything, he came down here and pushed us around and sneered at us and laughed at us and threw his weight about and told us how we'd always be poor nobodies while he would always be a rich somebody, and of course we couldn't do anything about it, what with him being an earl and all.'

Arthur nodded sympathetically; but said:

'Even so, Mr Futtergunk, that hardly excuses stealing his valuable diamond, surely?'

The little keeper's old eyes widened.

'Steal it?' he cried. 'I never *stole* it! I just sort of, well, borrowed it. I went down to Stepney with Tiddles, and –'

'Tiddles?' interrupted Doctor Watson. 'Funny name for a parrot.'

'Mrs Futtergunk always wanted a cat. Anyway, we went down to Pondicherry Villas – I'd been training Tiddles to fetch – and I just sort of let him off my shoulder, didn't I, and next thing I knew, he was back with the diamond.'

'Which you didn't return,' said Sherlock Holmes sternly.

'Not yet I haven't,' answered Mr Futtergunk. 'I planned to send it back anonymously after I'd taught Wilfred blooming Nutt a lesson. That's not a crime, is it?'

Nobody really wanted to answer that. Instead, Arthur said: 'Exactly what kind of lesson?'

'I'll show you,' replied Alfred J. Futtergunk, 'if you like.'

So they followed the elderly keeper outside. With the fog gone, and the late autumn sun up by now, it was a bright crisp day; just, in fact, the day for a stroll round the Zoo, which was why it was so crowded; but not, of course, why that crowd was laughing so hard that even the roars of the tigers and the shrieks of the cassowaries were utterly drowned out!

Everyone was standing outside the cages of the Ape House, laughing and pointing and chattering.

Holmes and Watson and Arthur pushed through the mob behind Mr Futtergunk, until they came to the barrier; and then they saw.

Inside the cage, grinning his enormous yellow teeth, and scratching his head, and jumping up and down with glee, was a little ginger chimpanzee.

Around his neck, on a scarlet ribbon, winking and flashing as it caught the bright rays of the early sun, was the Bellybutton Diamond!

But more than that. On a big card, wired to the middle of the cage-front just like all the other cards

which told visitors which particular animal they were looking at, was some writing, in large clear capital letters:

THE EARL OF STEPNEY, said the card, FORMERLY WILFRED NUTT OF TOOTING.

Alfred J. Futtergunk smiled gently.

'I just wanted to make a monkey out of him,' he said.

Well, of course, it was impossible for Sherlock Holmes and Doctor Watson and Arthur not to join in the laughter, especially as they all privately thought that this was just the thing to take the nasty Earl of Stepney down a peg or two. But a crime *had* been committed; there was no getting away from it.

'I suppose you're going to call the police now?' said Alfred J. Futtergunk, looking at Sherlock Holmes.

Holmes cleared his throat.

'It's, er, not my case any more,' he murmured. 'It's all up to Arthur.'

'That's a bit unfair!' protested Arthur, who certainly didn't want to be the one to have Mr Futtergunk put in prison. 'After all, Mr Holmes, you know much more about the law than I do. I mean, I'm not even sure exactly what *sort* of crime has been committed.'

Holmes turned suddenly, and fixed his glittering eye on Arthur.

'Precisely!' he cried. And the glittering eye winked. 'As far as a small boy like you knows, Arthur, this could well be a simple matter of, let us say, a naughty parrot taking what didn't belong to it, isn't that so?'

'I see,' said Arthur, for he did. 'And you couldn't very well call the police to arrest a parrot, could you? Especially when the parrot's owner had been brave enough to go into a monkey's cage, rescue the biggest diamond in the world, and return it to its grateful owner.'

'An interesting legal point,' said Sherlock Holmes, nodding. 'Of course, the parrot's owner would have to swear never to let his bird do that sort of thing again, wouldn't he, Mr Futtergunk?'

'Oh, yes, absolutely!' cried the delighted keeper.

'Added to which,' put in Doctor Watson, 'Arthur's client has been embarrassed enough already. Arthur would not be fair to the Earl of Stepney if he allowed the embarrassing facts to get into the newspapers, which would be bound to happen if the affair came to court, wouldn't it, Holmes?'

'Well said, Watson! An excellent point.'

'Thank you, Holmes,' replied the cheery doctor. He turned to Arthur. 'I think I deserve some sort of reward for making it, don't you, Arthur?'

'Reward?' said Arthur. 'What kind of reward?'

Doctor Watson patted his enormous stomach. 'GIVE US A PIECE OF CHEESE!' he said.

Other books from Puffin

THE PRIME MINISTER'S BRAIN
Gillian Cross

The fiendish DEMON HEADMASTER plans to gain control of No. 10 Downing Street and lure the Prime Minister into his evil clutches.

JASON BODGER AND THE PRIORY GHOST
Gene Kemp

A ghost story, both funny and exciting, about Jason, the bane of every teacher's life, who is pursued by the ghost of a little nun from the twelfth century!

HALFWAY ACROSS THE GALAXY AND TURN LEFT
Robin Klein

A humorous account of what happens to a family banished from their planet Zygron, when they have to spend a period of exile on Earth.

SUPER GRAN TO THE RESCUE
Forrest Wilson

The punchpacking, baddiebiffing escapades of the world's No. 1 senior citizen superhero – Super Gran! Now a devastating series on ITV!

TOM TIDDLER'S GROUND
John Rowe Townsend

Vic and Brain are given an old rowing boat which leads to the unravelling of a mystery and a happy reunion of two friends. An exciting adventure story.

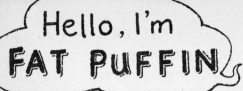

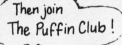

JELLYBEAN
Tessa Duder

A sensitive modern novel about Geraldine, alias 'Jellybean', who leads a rather solitary life as the only child of a single parent. She's tired of having to fit in with her mother's busy schedule, but a new friend and a performance of 'The Nut-cracker Suite' change everything.

THE PRIESTS OF FERRIS
Maurice Gee

Susan Ferris and her cousin Nick return to the world of O which they had saved from the evil Halfmen, only to find that O is now ruled by cruel and ruthless priests. Can they save the inhabitants of O from tryanny? An action-packed and gripping story by the author of prize-winning THE HALFMEN OF O.

THE SEA IS SINGING
Rosalind Kerven

In her seaside Shetland home, Tess is torn between the plight of the whales and loyalty to her father and his job on the oil rig. A haunting and thought-provoking novel.

BACK HOME
Michelle Magorian

A marvellously gripping story of an irrespressible girl's struggle to adjust to a new life. Twelve-year-old Rusty, who had been evacuated to the United States when she was seven, returns to the grey austerity of post-war Britain.

THE BEAST MASTER
André Norton

Spine-chilling science fiction – treachery and revenge! Host-een Storm is a man with a mission to find and punish Brad Quade, the man who killed his father long ago on Terra, the planet where life no longer exists.